# Pie in the Sky

Christine Moorcroft and Stefania Colnaghi

Evans

One fine day, Simon the Pieman
and his wife, Myra,
went for a ride on their bikes.

Simon had his eyes on the sky.
He spied something shiny
way up high.

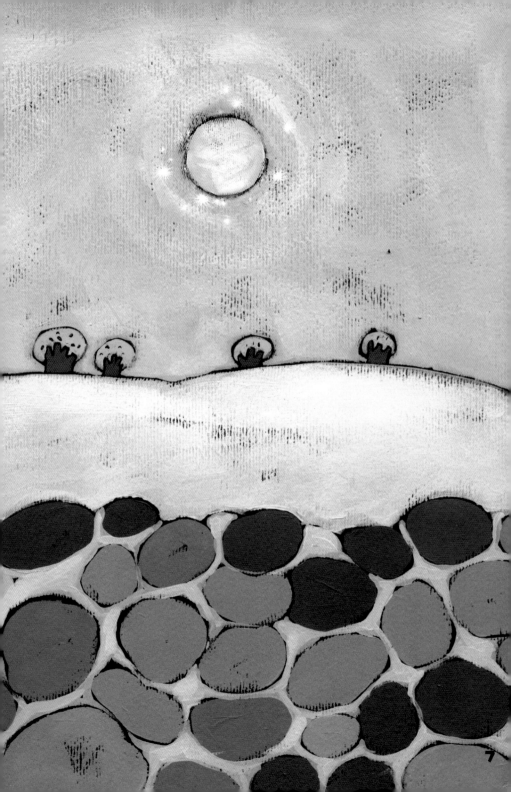

Myra spied it, too. She smiled. "It's nice and bright."

Simon wiped his eyes.
He was silent for a while.

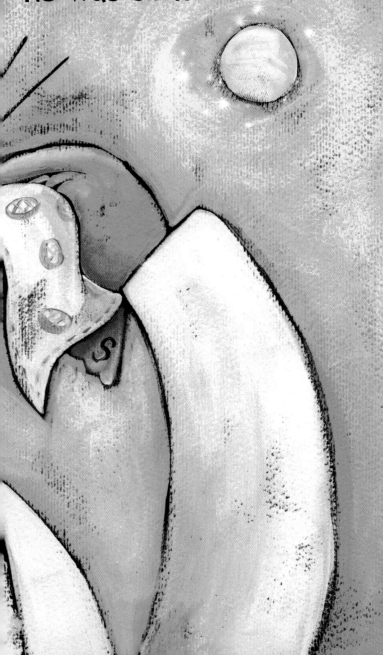

Then he cried,
"I spy a pie – a nice lime pie!"

12

"Slime pie!" cried Myra.
"How vile."

"Lime, not slime!" said Simon.

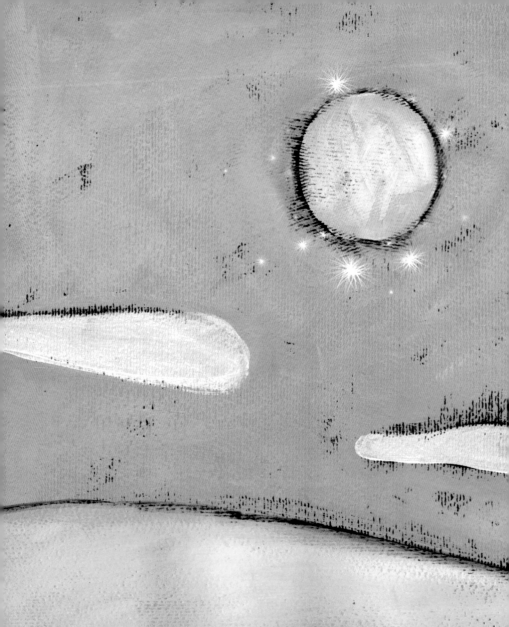

Myra was wiser than Simon.
"No, no. It isn't lime.
It's not a pie!"

"By my life, it's a pie,"
said Simon, getting wild.
"I'd like a slice.
Go and find a knife,
wife."

19

"It's a waste of time to try,"
replied his wife. "A knife
is tiny, the sky is miles high
and THERE IS NO PIE!"

Simon decided to stride
away from her side.
He had made up his mind.

"I'm going to climb,"
he said with pride.
"It's worth a try.
The pie will be mine."

Myra tried to hide her smile.
She sat down by a stile
to rest for a while.

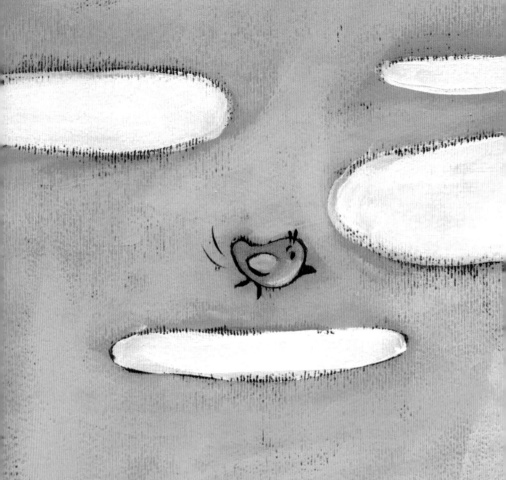

Meanwhile Simon tried and tried
to find the pie.
How did it hide?

"Wait until tonight," sighed Myra. "You'll see why there's no pie in the sky.

It's really the moon you silly buffoon."

**Twisters Rhymers** follow on from the success of the **Twisters** series. Twisters are gripping short stories from different genres, told in just 50 words, with an appealing choice of illustration styles and content. Why not try one?

**Not-so-silly Sausage** by Stella Gurney and Liz Million 978 0237 52875 1
**Nick's Birthday** by Jane Oliver and Silvia Raga 978 0237 52896 6
**Out Went Sam** by Nick Turpin and Barbara Nascimbeni 978 0237 52894 2
**Yummy Scrummy** by Paul Harrison and Belinda Worsley 978 0237 52876 8
**Squelch!** by Kay Woodward and Stefania Colnaghi 978 0237 52895 9
**Sally Sails the Seas** by Stella Gurney and Belinda Worsley 978 0237 52893 5
**Billy on the Ball** by Paul Harrison and Silvia Raga 978 0237 52926 0
**Countdown** by Kay Woodward and Ofra Amit 978 0237 52927 7
**One Wet Welly** by Gill Matthews and Belinda Worsley 978 0237 52928 4
**Sand Dragon** by Su Swallow and Silvia Raga 978 0237 52929 1
**Cave-baby and the Mammoth** by Vivian French and Lisa Williams 978 0237 52931 4
**Albert Liked Ladders** by Su Swallow and Tim Archbold 978 0237 52930 7
**Molly is New** by Nick Turpin and Silvia Raga 978 0237 53067 9
**A Head Full of Stories** by Su Swallow and Tim Archbold 978 0237 53069 3
**Elephant Rides Again** by Paul Harrison and Liz Million 978 0237 53073 0
**Bird Watch** by Su Swallow and Simona Dimitri 978 0237 53071 6
**Pip Likes Snow** by Lynne Rickards and Belinda Worsley 978 0237 53075 4
**How to Build a House** by Nick Turpin and Barbara Nascimbeni 978 0237 53065 5
**Hattie the Dancing Hippo** by Jillian Powell and Emma Dodson 978 0237 53335 9
**Mary Had a Dinosaur** by Eileen Browne and Ruth Rivers 978 0237 53337 3
**When I Was a Baby** by Madeline Goodey and Amy Brown 978 0237 53334 2
**Will's Boomerang** by Stella Gurney and Stefania Colnaghi 978 0237 53336 6
**Birthday Boy** by Dereen Taylor and Ruth Rivers 978 0237 53469 1
**Mr Bickle and the Ghost** by Stella Gurney and Silvia Raga 978 0237 53465 3
**Noisy Books** by Paul Harrison and Fabiano Fiorin 978 0237 53467 7
**Undersea Adventure** by Paul Harrison and Barbara Nascimbeni 978 0237 53463 9